CW00400302

HORROR ST
TO TELL IN THE DARK

BOOK 2

SHORT SCARY HORROR STORIES

ANTHOLOGY FOR

TEENAGERS AND YOUNG ADULTS

BRYCE NEALHAM

Copyright © by Bryce Nealham.

All rights reserved. No part of this publication may be reproduced, distributed, or transmitted in any form or by any means, including photocopying, recording, or other electronic or mechanical methods, or by any information storage and retrieval system without the prior written permission of the publisher, except in the case of very brief quotations embodied in critical reviews and certain other noncommercial uses permitted by copyright law.

This is a work of fiction. Names, characters, business, events and incidents are the products of the author's imagination. Any resemblance to actual persons, living or dead, or actual events is purely coincidental.

CONTENTS

Find Out About Our Latest Horror Book Releases...

Simply go to the URL below and you will be notified as soon as a new book has been launched.

bit.ly/3q34yte

"Believe nothing you hear, and only one half that you see."

— Edgar Allan Poe

STRANDED

By Maya Scianna

My feet were submerged in 14 inches of wet snow. The sky was black with scattered stars and a crescent moon being my only light source besides my car's bright lights that reflected off of the snow that was falling all around me.

Due to the number of car crashes on the highway, I had to take side roads to get home from my college campus. I thought I would make it in time, but the snow decided not to cooperate with me that day.

I got back into my car and tried to warm up again. I took off my socks and shoes and saw that my feet were white and my toes were bright red.

I grabbed the duffel bag that I called "my winter safety kit", unfortunately, I couldn't get my car to move at all. Ice had wedged in between my tires and prevented them from gaining traction.

I cried in frustration, putting my head down on my steering wheel, sounding the horn. There wasn't anyone around for miles, but I still hoped that somehow someone driving nearby would hear it. I laid my car seat back as far as it could go and leaned against it.

As I was about to call for a tow truck, my eyes met pale skin, shoulder-length brown hair, and small grey eyes staring back at me. She stood in front of my car, her legs buried in the snow and snowflakes sitting on her eyelashes and hair.

She stood there in a stained purple t-shirt with a pink flower in the center of it and jeans. She looked to be around 6 years old.

What concerned me most were her blue lips and frail body. I grabbed my extra jacket out of the duffel bag and went to go help the girl. Then she was gone.

I looked around, trying to see through the thick air. My stomach twisted itself and a slimy feeling slithered up my spine. I roamed around a bit. What was she doing outside all by herself? What if she dies out here?

I tried to use my phone flashlight, but it was completely useless. "Hey! Where did you go?" I called out into the night.

I trudged forward a little farther, trying to look around better, but all I could see was white flakes of snow and fog. I eventually had to give up and go back to my car.

She was in the passenger seat with the side door open, snow piled up on her lap, and the floor of my car. My heart leaped out of my chest but I forced it back in.

I hesitantly got back into my car and tried to hand her my extra jacket that was now covered in a thin blanket of snow. She didn't take it. Instead, she stared up at me with her grey eyes that looked right through me.

Maybe she was nervous and scared. I shivered. "We'll get you home hopefully tomorrow, okay?" She didn't respond. "Uh, are you hungry? I have granola bars in my purse." Nothing. I went to try and shut her door and she gripped my arm and shoved it away.

Then she just got out of my car and I tried to stop her, forcing myself through the snow to make it over to her. "Wait, stop!"

Then she started running towards the forest, kicking up the snow behind her and somehow managing to keep her balance. My mind and body were in conflict.

My mind was telling me to ditch the child and go back to my car, but my body was complying with the little girl and running after her.

The conflict came to a halt when we ended up at a lit-up house in the open field that was surrounded by trees. I'd thought there wasn't anything for miles. Why was she in the middle of the road? Did she hear my car horn? I wondered.

I watched her run up the steps and through the open door. I heard the faintest little voice, "Come in." I was extremely cold and was worried about getting frostbite, so I went over and peered through the doorway before stepping inside.

I shut the door behind me and stood on the welcome mat at the door with my sopping wet sneakers.

"Hello?" I was met with silence. I took off my wet shoes and socks to avoid tracking snow through their home. It was a brightly lit home that fit the stereotypical suburb family home.

Everything fit a brown and tan color scheme, it had a family feel to it, but something felt a little off.

There was a putrid smell coming from the kitchen, so I went to see if someone was in there. "Hello?" I said again.

The kitchen was empty except for a pot on the stove boiling over with a thick, black liquid. Warning bells went off in my head and I immediately turned around and went back towards the front door. What the hell was going on?

Thump. I stopped and gazed up at the staircase and saw the little girl. When we made eye contact she started running. I needed to take her to the police station. No one was here, and there was something odd going on.

I ran in the direction the girl ran and found a bedroom with purple crayon drawings all over a white wooden door. I assumed it was the little girl's room, and opened it.

This room was different from the rest. I was hit with the smell of death. Blood dripped down from the ceiling down the lilac purple walls and onto the floor, turning the light tan carpet a reddish-brown.

A breeze pushed through shredded pink curtains. Bloody and torn limbs were littered around the bedroom. Bloody fingers, feet, and hands were mangled. Chunks of flesh and bone hung off each limb. I felt bile rise in my stomach and force its way onto the carpet.

"Oh god," I said out loud.

Crack. My body spun around to find the little girl staring up with me, her jaw open and slightly askew, Thick, dark blood pouring from her once grey eyes that look as if they were filled with black ink, and her head snapped to the side at an unnatural angle. She was a monster waiting for me to make the first move.

So I did.

I thought about the open window and immediately made a run for it, but before I could I felt tiny bony arms and hands wrap around my leg, pulling me down.

My skull has met the windowsill and everything went white. I tried to get into a sitting position, but my skull started pounding for a second. Adrenaline was shooting through every part of my body trying to get me to run for my life, but I could barely open my eyes.

I sat up and tried to adjust my eyes to the room again, but then felt something wet slide down the top of my foot. I opened my eyes and I saw something that would haunt me for the rest of my life.

The tiny monster that sat in front of me had taken a knife and was slicing off my toes one by one with a kitchen knife, she was already slicing the third.

My screams filled the house, but she didn't seem to notice or care. I used my other foot to kick her and to try and escape. The sides of her mouth turned upward, revealing yellow-stained sharp razor teeth.

She slithered on top of me and held me down as I screamed until her face was in mine. Her breath was rancid, and blood, my blood, dripped down her chin and landed on my cheek.

I started kicking, the pain on my foot muted by adrenaline. I ended up kicking one of the limbs lying on the carpet nearby and the girl turned around like a wild animal and chased after it before chewing on it.

I pulled myself off the floor, onto the window ledge, and leaped out the window, and landed in the fresh, powdered snow.

Crack. I'd landed on my foot incorrectly, unfortunately, now both of my feet were in pain but again, adrenaline helped me take off running barefoot through the snow faster than I'd ever run in my entire life.

I didn't look back to see if I was being followed, but I did hear the sounds of screeching and wailing from behind me.

I got into my car heaving and coughing, my hair completely knotted and my foot leaving trails of blood. I locked all of the car doors, started the car, turned the heat and headlights back on, dialed called 911.

"Please…a child" I stuttered out, "at an empty house just" I paused, not knowing exactly what to say, " just tried to- kill me" I gasped, still struggling to breathe.

Needless to say, they were very confused and concerned. I

explained how I'd gotten to where I was, and they were able to locate me. They said they couldn't get there with the heavy snowfall but they'd call a tow. It would take hours.

I hung up and started to cry. What if she came back?

She did come back. Only she watched me from in front of the car. She looked normal again, except her eyes narrowed.

A drop of blood dripped down from her eye and froze on her skin. I could only watch as she jumped onto the hood of my car with her face only separated by the windshield. I was frozen,

I didn't know what to do. I was trapped. The monster smacked her head into the windshield.

Crack. Blood flowed down the glass and crystallized.

Crack. The car wobbled and a fissure formed.

Crack. Blood was trapped in the fissures of the car,

I grabbed my ice scraper out of the backseat. *Crash.* Glass shards exploded and landed in parts of my face and arms.

I swung the metal part of the scraper as hard I could against her skull and watched in horror as she let out the most horrific scream that filled my ears with ringing. I swung again and she stumbled forward, almost falling on top of me.

She reached her hand out and tried to grab the scraper from me but I was able to dodge it.

An animalistic growl erupted from her and I hit her again and pushed her backward, sending her tumbling down the front of my car and landing in the snow.

I laid back onto my seat, refusing to look at her. I didn't have any fight left in me. My eyes and skin stung. My lungs burned as they tried to inhale.

Is she dead? I wondered. I wasn't sure I wanted to go and find out.

I pulled my red fuzzy blanket from the backseat and covered myself with it, not caring if blood, snow, and dirt was getting all over it. A small sob escaped my throat.

Bright lights reflected off of the snow and glittered. There was a tow truck heading towards me. I was overcome with a sense of relief and warmth filling my body. I was saved, I was alive.

The next day, police searched the area and found nothing; just an empty clearing in the forest. I'd taken pictures of my car and myself and sent them in as evidence, and they were extremely confused and concerned.

I tried to go back to my normal life, trying to pretend as nothing happened. Weeks went by. I was avoiding those side roads and taking the highway to and from my college classes.

That was until one day the police knocked on my door and started questioning me about the experience again. Turns out, they'd found a trail of limbs from that part of the forest, leading directly to my house.

ABOUT THE AUTHOR

Maya Scianna

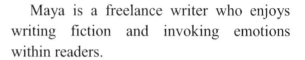

Maya is a freelance writer who enjoys writing fiction and invoking emotions within readers.

She mostly ghostwrites content for websites but will jump on the opportunity to write fiction stories, especially thrillers.

She currently has a website where she keeps a portfolio of stories she's written and a blog where she shares tips and her writing process.

When she's not writing, she's either reading, binging TV shows on Netflix, playing video games on her Switch, or looking for a new place to travel to.

You can reach Maya through her website: www.mscreative.online

Alternatively, her email is mayabree@gmail.com

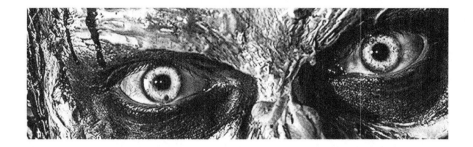

SKINS

By Britney Supernault

The first one popped up on September 25.

Three teenagers had found what looked like a destroyed leather suitcase on the old Sac's trail near the school. It wouldn't be until they rolled it over, did they discover the awful truth.

The two boys and one girl were two grades ahead of me and were set to graduate that year. However, after the incident they all dropped out.

That day, the police arrived on the scene 25 minutes after the phone call was made. The entire school, however, was there in 15. The magic of being a teenager with social media and living in a small midwestern town where nothing seemed to happen.

I didn't go that day.

I sometimes wish that I had.

The rest of my schoolmates, however, were there in a flurry of curiosity.

In the play-by-plays I heard all the next day, they smelt it far before they saw it. One girl, Jenny Arkins was still pale green as she recounted to the class what the smell was like. Putrid, sick, filling up her nostrils with how she thought bile would smell.

Anthony Parry took up the story from there while tears spilled from the blonde-haired Jenny's eyes and her friends took her away from the lunch table.

He said that he was one of the first there (he was the school track-and-field star, after all, he noted) and after pushing past the group of three who discovered it, standing like planted trees over the mess, did his stomach drop like a rock into a pond.

He didn't know what it was at first – it looked like a moldy suitcase that had fallen apart, or maybe some silicone costume of some sort, but his instinct told him to look further.

"Turn it over," said one of the first three there, Jenny Arkin's older sister, Lisa. The one who would be gone before the end of the year.

His eyes glossed over at the lunch table. His fork stuck in the space between his uneaten lunch and his open mouth.

The bell gave a shrill ring, jolting me from my spot and forcing me and everyone else to get up and move towards the trash cans.

 After being jostled by other kids, also talking about the day before, I made it to the door of the cafeteria. I looked behind me and saw Anthony still perched perfectly still on his seat, staring off into nothing, eyes shiny like glass, alone in the emptying cafeteria.

I heard the rest of the story in history. The teacher sat at the desk, head resting on her hand and brow knitted together deep in thought. The rest of the class gathered towards the back, surrounding Michael Hems who was retelling what he had seen.

He said that he got there minutes after the police showed up. He almost didn't get a look at it through the large crowd of teenagers craning their necks to get a peek past the police.

They were shutting the area down, yellow tape going up by the roll. Michael had heard a loud gasp from the girl beside him and he turned his gaze to where her eyes had landed – a small space between the parked police cruisers.

It was leathery, the color of a corkboard, and looked stretched out. He had been confused at first, but when his eyes traveled further, he dropped his cell phone out of his hands.

A face.

A human face at the end of the leather.

A girl fainted in the class.

The school made an announcement. Afternoon classes were canceled. We were all dismissed.

The next day the coroner's office made a statement. The thing found in the forest was in fact, human remains. Skin. A pile of skin with the face still intact.

The next week was nothing but shocked silence. Stores closed early, teachers stared off into space, and the only conversation at dinner tables that week was on the thing found in the forest. Police cars were seen in and around the old Sac's trail.

The police were attempting to identify the remains. My mom had to change her running route.

But sooner than later, life returned to normal. Halloween was approaching in less than a week and the conversations turned to costumes. Characters from this year's most popular movies, classic ghost sheets, and some of the more stupid kids joked about going as bags of skins.

The three teenagers who had originally found the remains didn't return to school yet. Jenny Arkins began skipping classes.

"I have to support my sister. She's..." She trailed off while quietly speaking to me at her locker. Her eyes never met mine and she was quickly out the door with her textbooks clutched closely to her chest.

It was around Halloween that the feeling began. It was the day of, to be exact. My mother had a late shift and couldn't take my little sister trick-or-treating, so I was left with babysitting duty. I didn't mind – it meant at least a quarter of the spoils.

I took her down the usual candy route, aiming to hit the best houses for the biggest chocolate bars. She ran ahead with a classmate, and they quickly left me a couple of houses behind.

It was hard to ignore that more houses were dark this year than in years past. I watched one house in particular; a large white house with dusty windows and an old tree that was gnarled so much that it almost bent downwards.

There was an intriguing emptiness to it that seemed to call to me. I had never noticed it in all the decade that I had gone down this same candy route.

A small breeze blew by, gently caressing my neck as if someone were right behind me. Instantly the hair on my arms and neck stood up in alarm as a wheezing, grasping inhale was heard right behind my ear.

I swung around with my arms raised, ready to yell at whoever the hell was standing so close to me. But my arms hit only the cool, fall air.

I was alone on the street.

Only the distant sound of kids screaming in delight could be heard. Instead, I was facing the Birchwood forest that stood at erect attention, bare branches swaying gently in the breeze that had just chilled me to the bone.

I squinted my eyes in an attempt to see if there was any scurrying figure of a jerk teenage looking to scare me, but all my eyes were met with was the deep dark curtain of shadow behind the first row of trees. I shook off the nervousness with an uneasy chuckle. I had just freaked myself out.

And that's what I continued to tell myself. Even when for the rest of the night, I couldn't shake the feeling that I was being watched.

Even when the next pile of skin was found. And the news anchor reported the location as being exactly where I was looking on that Halloween eve.

That should have been when I realized something was happening.

The town went into a state of alarming panic. A new curfew, no after-school activities, and police regularly patrolling the parks were the new town protocol.

Everyone walked with a wary eye towards the person next to them. My sister came home with new words in her vocabulary like 'serial killer', 'aliens', and 'cult'.

Our town name was now internationally recognized. New faces began to show up. Suddenly, in the town where nothing happened, something startling was beginning.

The third one showed up three weeks later. Except this one was different. Where the others had been old, shredded, and nearly unrecognizable, this one seemed...newer.

The coroner came back quickly with the results – these were the remains of a missing person case from one state over. When we heard, my mother's face was contorted in a myriad of what looked like shock, confusion, and something I had never seen in her face before: fear.

No matter how bad it got, I still wanted to go to school. Where other parents had pulled their kids out of school and moved to a different town, I wanted to stay.

When I saw my mother searching for jobs in other states, I convinced her that she was overreacting. Whether it was morbid fascination, or I was excited to be in the middle of international action, I was set on staying.

I never told my mother about the sounds.

The raspy breaths I would hear in the corner of my room. Or the feeling of eyes on my back as I walked to school.

In a way, perhaps I was fascinated by the morbidity of the fact that something new was happening to me. Finally.

The fourth one came. These remains even newer than the last. They quickly traced the skin to a missing person's case about 3 hours south.

"They're getting closer." My mother would say to herself.

"Maybe they're already here." I would reply. A breathy rasp could be heard in the wind.

More faces showed up in our town. Suddenly, the restaurants and cafes were filled with a colorful crowd of reporters, paranormal investigators, and those wanting to see the train wreck up close and personal. A shaky inhale from the corner of the booth.

At night, an eerie green light began to fill my dreams. The people in my dreams, my mom and sister and classmates, would begin to waver, growing more and more unsteady, like a reflection in a pond that was suddenly touched. Soon they would melt off and in their place was... something. I never got to that part.

A phone call was made to my mom. I hadn't handed in an assignment in over a month.

14

"I didn't know I had any assignments," I told my mom whose face was slowly growing more haggard as time passed. Everyone was just waiting for the next pile. She waved me away.

The eyes never left my back. Instead, they had almost become a close friend, a companion. I would intentionally walk through the forest. I wasn't entirely sure why.

Tragedy had hit the town. A teenage girl had taken her life. Filled her schoolbag with rocks and went for a stroll in the river valley. Only the clothes and schoolbag were found with a help of a dive team. I went to the spot where she had supposedly made the plunge. I swear I could feel the breath right on my shoulder. The now, familiar shaky intake of breath.

"Almost..." the wind spoke quietly in a sing-song voice.

"Almost..." I whisper quietly before turning back.

Sale signs lined my street. My sister could only fall asleep in my mother's bed. I preferred the dark now. My own breath aligned with the one in the corner.

The fifth one came a few days before Christmas. This one was more familiar to the police. The hair was still attached, blonde. The police made the announcement a few days later. Lisa Arkins had apparently not killed herself.

"Oh...my..." My mother cried out.

"Finally," I spoke. She turned to face me, and her face contorted in horror. My skin was too itchy.

I began to claw and claw and claw. My mother tried to stop my hands but couldn't.

"What are you doing?!" She cried out. I turned and walked out the door, my little sister screaming behind me.

My skin was much too itchy now.

I walked and walked and walked. My vision was now completely green.

"Next" whispered the wind.

"Next" I spoke back to nothing. To everything. I followed the raspy breath. Down my street. My hands were now red. But the itch was almost gone.

I walked up to the Birchwood forest. Past the white house, the figure in the window waved.

I raised my hand with a wave before turning towards the forest, leaving my skin in front of the Birchwood trees.

ABOUT THE AUTHOR

Britney Supernault

Britney Supernault, also known as the Cree Nomad, hails from the wintery north of Alberta, Canada. Coming from the small community of East Prairie Metis Settlement, Britney is proud of her Métis Cree background and settlement but is most often seen out of country.

An avid traveler, Cree Nomad is an experienced freelance writer, specializing in travel articles, but hopes to expand into the world of fiction by becoming an author herself. She hopes to publish her first novel in the next two years.

Having written and delivered over 120 articles this year alone, Britney prides herself as being 'the most determined writer you will ever meet'. Working mainly through the freelancing platforms Fiverr and Upwork, you can find the Cree Nomad seated at a café in some faraway country with a coffee in hand and her eyes trained on her laptop.

You can read more of her work in her personal blog at Creenomad.com, or by visiting her Instagram page: Cree_Nomad.

If you'd like to hire her for any articles, blog posts, or your ghostwriting needs, feel free to contact her through her Fiverr or Upwork profiles, or email her at: thecreenomad@gmail.com.

IN THE TREE

By Frederick Trinidad

My mom runs a business of sending domestic helpers abroad and as part of the applicants' training and assessment; she would initially have them work in our house in exchange for fair local salaries.

Since a lot of them came from the countryside, they would sometimes share stories about paranormal encounters and supernatural beings stemming from each of their respective suburban villages.

Each of their stories never failed to both fascinate and frighten me and my siblings.

Though my younger siblings find their stories cripplingly frightening, I was old enough to know that those stories were nothing more than myths and legends.

Or so I thought.

In one of the many instances that our mother hired new house helps, one stood among the rest.

I can't remember her name so let's just call her Rebecca.

The reason I said that she stood above the rest isn't because she is pretty nor does she possess a certain air of mystery about her. No, she stood out because the man who lives in the tree took a liking to her.

If you ask me to clarify the preposition used in that sentence, I wouldn't know.

Because I never saw him.

I never knew whether he lived inside or outside that tree. But what I do know and will never forget, are the things he apparently did to Rebecca.

The tree in question is a Muntingia tree standing at the far end corner of our garden and it has always been there for as long as I could remember.

It peacefully stood there and my brothers occasionally climb it to collect some of its sweet, delicious berries.

The one dog that we had always barked at it for whatever reason but we were quick to brush it off, given the fact that he liked to bark at almost everything.

At one time or another, we even tied a swing and a hammock onto its branches during hot summer days due to the effective cooling shades of its bountiful leaves.

And except for the one incident when my older brother accidentally fell from it and injured his wrist, nothing significant ever came from the tree.

And yes, that is until Rebecca entered the scene.

When she first arrived, the maids would often tease her for never having a boyfriend.

Despite being in her late 20's, she said she just couldn't find the right guy to be her future husband.

Later, the rest of the household started noticing Rebecca spending a lot of her free time around the tree. She would spend hours upon hours just seating on the swing connected to it and singing songs everybody else could barely hear.

Every day, she would studiously go about her assigned tasks, disengaging in casual conversations with her colleagues.

She started sparing lesser and lesser attention to her own hygiene and nourishment.

Her isolation ever increased and she would spend her rest days just frolicking around the tree. The entire household started to worry about her mental state and by the time news reached my mom, it seemed already too late.

My mom tried firing her and arranging for her to be shipped back to her province but she strongly resisted.

She insisted she'd stay and work for free, canceling her contract to go abroad.

Together with the rest of the household, they were still figuring out their next step when our mother had to leave on short notice for an important business trip overseas.

She would be gone for an entire month and left the tenure housemaids in charge of the house.

One night, like we often did, I and my siblings were having dinner together with the house helps. Like any normal dinner night, there was laughter, teasing, and conversation shared across the table.

Rebecca was just eating quietly on her side of the table when she suddenly fell from her chair.

She was crying on the floor as her colleagues tried to comfort her and tried to learn what just happened.

Then we noticed it.

A reddish, discernable handprint lay across the left side of her face.

While the possibility of her slapping her own face was relevant, the print was far too large to derive from her own puny hands.

And we were all there talking while eating, so it would be a fair assumption to think we would have seen her, or someone else, slapping her on the face.

It was the first of the series of mysterious incidents that would happen in our house. They pressed her for answers until she finally admitted what happened.

She was in a relationship with the being that exists in or on the tree. And he slapped her because he was angry that she might leave him.

We were all very shaken up by the event that everyone decided to retire together in the servants' quarters.

The eldest of the housemaids, with all her folklore wisdom, finally questioned Rebecca and slowly unfolded the events which followed that evening.

She first investigated Rebecca on her knowledge of the underworld.

What frightened me the most is that both lady's knowledge of the supernatural and Rebecca's stories were closely matching up.

The story goes is that the tree is actually a portal to another world. The way they described it, is that the other world closely resembles the fairy tale worlds found in children's books.

People of very attractive looks adorned in very ornamental garments populate these worlds.

If one took passage onto the human world and develops a liking for one of its inhabitants, they tend to lure someone into their world through undeniable temptations.

If you are one of the very few who were lucky enough to be invited to visit their world, then feel free to honor them with your presence.

But if you wish to return to your own world, there is but one rule; never consume their food.

You would be offered the most delectable, most delicious-looking food you have ever seen.

Even if you feel the least bit hungry, upon landing sight of the food, you would magically feel excruciating hunger, making you want to eat your fill.

But you must not eat.

Not one bite of fruit, not one grain of rice.

For if you do, you'd slowly turn away from your world and permanently live among them.

And despite having this knowledge, Rebecca ate.

She then admitted to having grown tired of this world and wanting to go to their world.

But the moment she took the first bite of her food, the world started revealing the reality beneath its lies.

The people turned into nasty-looking gargoyles, her prince-charming boyfriend turned into an ugly 12-foot naked man sporting a hideous face, the food turned into stones, and the fairy tale castle turned into a dark monumental cave filled with bat-like creatures holding on to giant stalactites.

Worst still, there was a feeling of extreme loneliness enveloping her heart. She quickly excused herself and hurriedly went back to the human world.

But even after going back from the horrid dimension, there seemed to be no escape for her.

Slowly, she was being dragged back into their world.

The very slap on her face, while she's in the human world, is the undeniable evidence of it. Rebecca's actions became more erratic the following days and we would often see marks and bruises upon her.

Our mom was away on business when it was all happening and I wasn't aware if she was given knowledge as to what's going on in the house.

It was our summer vacation from school, therefore; we could not help but witness and be part of the horror that was happening in our home.

Luckily my siblings were still too young to comprehend that there's something very amiss happening around us. Everybody moved in pairs and the children, including me, were never left alone.

A medium was called in.

Rebecca, the elder lady, and several maids were gathered to perform what I could only describe as a séance.

I remember that none of the children were allowed in the servants' quarters where the ritual was apparently being performed. We were all kept along with some of the staff members in the living room.

My youngest brother later asked me and one of the maids to accompany him to the kitchen because he wanted some snacks.

I was weary.

The room where the séance was being performed is right next to the kitchen.

And then, a loud shriek emanated from the room.

The sound seemed to be a mixture of painful screams and the wailing of women. My little brother's curiosity overtook his fears and he dashed for the servants' quarters.

The maid stood dumbfounded in her tracks and I took off running after my brother. But he beat me to it.

He swung the door open and just stood frozen to whatever he was witnessing. I caught up with him with the intention of grabbing and pulling him back to safety, but I inevitably witnessed what he discovered.

The group of seated women gathered themselves into a circle with a lit candlestick in their midst. They didn't seem to notice our presence.

With closed eyes, they were holding hands and murmuring words I could barely hear and understand.

And Rebecca, she was not seated among the group. She was standing atop a table stand located on the corner of the room, facing the wall.

Her head was slightly tilted to her side which gave the impression of her being hanged by a rope connected to the ceiling.

But there was no rope.

Her long, distinctive hair should have been resting on the left side of her shoulder but it was resting upon her back as though her head wasn't tilted.

Worst still, her waist was bent to a forward unnatural position like she was about to give birth or defecate while standing up.

It was, no doubt, the strangest thing I ever saw. I stood there frozen in fear and trepidation. It was my turn to stand dumbfounded as to what was going on.

The medium all of a sudden broke her meditation and started screaming at us to get out.

I was pulled back to reality and I quickly took my brother out of the room and closed the door behind us. I carried my brother and run for the living room and we stayed there for the entirety of the night.

I could not wrap my head around the things that I and my brother witnessed that evening. I couldn't sleep but at the same time, I thank God for the innocence beholding my little brother.

Because like any given night, he slept peacefully unwary of the horrific occurrences in our once peaceful home.

The following days were met with the elder lady escorting Rebecca to the tree each night, making offers of food and prayers by its roots.

The strangest thing about this was, the food they leave each night would be gone the next day.

When my mom went back, her reaction upon gaining knowledge about the recent, fantastical events was disgust towards how the crazy events were handled by those she left in charge of the house.

She dismissed all the crazy, supernatural bullshit and took complete control of the situation. Her biggest concern was how the whole thing affected us, her children.

But upon learning that we barely understood and cared about what was going on, she was relieved.

At least that's what I told her for my part.

Our strong-willed mother settled things down completely by taking full charge of the house, relocating all the current house helps and taking in a fresh new batch of applicants.

She then checked Rebecca into a mental health care facility.

Only a few months would go by and Rebecca seemed to heal and was healthy enough to resume her plans of working abroad.

Nothing remotely scary happened in the house after that, we moved home after a few years and I studied college and work like everyone else.

I'll never know if Rebecca was healed by the séance, the elder's nightly ritual, or by the medical procedures done to her in the health care facility.

I never heard of anything more about Rebecca. But I would never forget what my little brother told me that faithful evening.

Before falling asleep, he told me that Rebecca wasn't standing atop a table stand.

No, she was raised from the ground by an ugly, tall man with one of his hands wrapped around her neck.

DESTITUTE

By Frederick Trinidad

"I am a failure."

That was all I could think of while staring down the hollow barrel of a gun. Both my hands clutched tightly upon the handle as I prepared to end my miserable existence.

"How did I even afford to get this gun?" I thought to myself.

"This is stupid. I don't need this gun; a knife should suffice". I continued to think as I pondered upon my life-ending decision.

And for whatever reason, I suddenly thought of a story I read about a lost mountain climber rescued only a day after he decided to succumb to the inevitable.

There was still a tiny piece of chocolate bar in his pocket, and there was no way he would die with food still on him.

The brutal cold of the snow-ridden mountain has fully seeped into his winter clothes, and both his arms were already stiff from being frozen.

He had to summon all his remaining strength to reach down his back pocket and retrieve the life-giving supplement.

He then found a spot beneath a dead tree in what he accepted to be his final resting place.

He ate the morsel and then became as comfortable as possible before closing his eyes and slipping into oblivion.

By some miracle, a couple of hikers happened upon him the next day, and despite his seemingly unconscious state, he was still alive.

He was rescued and now hailed as an inspiring survivor who has proven humanities' relentless will to live.

Or, at least that's how the media portrayed him. The way I see it, he was just damn lucky. He was ready to die and have fully submitted himself to the other side, whatever that is.

Then I compared my gun to his chocolate bar. There was no way I was going to kill myself while still having the ability to buy food.

And I thought, maybe, just maybe. A miracle could happen for me as well. That's what I decided on that day.

As you may have already guessed, I was a bum; a failure in life. I am an old, homeless wanderer who couldn't afford to stay in a single place for too long.

I even had to exchange my worn-out duffel bag for a few packets of food; thus, I secured all my belongings in a proper garbage bag. I would later do the same thing with my gun.

That improvised armament was the only thing I had left that still held some monetary value. I exchanged it for an amount which was enough to see me fed for about a week.

But the fact that I hated most in this life is having to deal with other people.

They avoid me as I walk past them.

They may think I'm too poor and stupid to understand what makes me a vile figure in their eyes.

But I do know why.

People are judgmental.

They judge me by the odor I exude, the ragged clothes on my back, and the dirt upon my face.

I am very sick of it and yet, I know their actions were justified. Nevertheless, it's all the same crap that I experience on a daily basis.

The following days went by as uneventful as they always did. I traveled upon seemingly the same roads; I sat on seemingly the same pavements. They were different places but to me, they're all the same cold, unwelcoming environment in which I lived for most of my life.

Each night, before submitting myself to another restless sleep, I always check the elements around my surroundings. Certain of the fact that my looks and clothing would never betray me to anyone who wishes to rob someone.

The very shoes I wear have gaping holes in them, thus stealing them would be a lot more trouble than their worth.

My sickly and elderly appearance dictates that my noxious internal organs would not be profitable for those who may think to steal and sell them.

Somehow, I was able to rest knowing that my outward inferiority actually shielded me from those malicious intents. Sadly, that isn't the case for some of the healthier, younger creatures of the night.

I've been cursed to see a few of them forcibly taken by grown, sturdy men. Fearing for our lives, none of us would dare interfere with those men.

We were all indigents who have accepted that such atrocities were among the cost of leaving on the streets.

We knew that the kidnapped women would become sex slaves and the men were taken to be killed for their internal organs. Thinking about it, my nerves would strain towards such evil injustice.

Hey, I now remember how I got my gun.

Allow me to take a pause and tell you how I got it.

It happened many years ago on a rainy evening when I tried helping a man whose daughter was being taken.

The father was desperately pleading with the kidnappers to take him instead while pulling his daughter by the arm in a vain attempt of retrieving her back from the evil men.

I was nearby and I instinctively helped the man take back his daughter by pulling her by the other arm. The next thing I heard was a loud bang from a gun as a result of discharging a bullet.

The father was shot squarely on the head and he was dead before hitting the ground.

With my hand still clutching the girl's arm, the shooter turned towards me. His bloodshot eyes widened their gaze upon me as if they were about to pop and fall off his face.

A distinctive scar running across his ugly mug wrinkled as he menacingly pointed the gun towards my face and hurriedly squeezed the trigger.

But it was not my time yet.

The gun jammed and I impulsively let go of the girl's arm and run for the nearest corner. I heard the gun go off but the bullet missed me.

As I cowered behind a thick bush, I heard another gunfire as the man continued shooting at me.

Fearing that the gunshots may have alerted people of authority nearby, the man abandoned his quest of killing me. They shoved the girl into a van and drove off speedily into the night.

I went back to the crime scene and helplessly stared at the poor, lifeless man as the heavy rain washed the blood off him as though washing him off the sins of this world.

People of equal standing started gathering around the corpse knowing that justice is not to be expected despite the monstrosity of the crime. We have witnessed our kind falling victim to the same sort of crime but very seldom is justice served.

Despite all the witnesses, all the evidence, and every bit of available details that's more than enough to permanently take away the perpetrators, there would be no justice.

I moved my eyes to see the abandoned gun lying across the pavement. That criminal may have dropped it accidentally as he and his companions scramble to flee the area.

Those men didn't even care to retrieve the gun which could be used as evidence against them. Heck, they were so confident that society and justice holds no regard for people like us, they didn't even care to use face masks.

I picked up the gun and placed it inside my duffel bag and walked away, never to discover what the events of that evening would ultimately arrive at.

I could never fathom my body's audacity to continue living under such morose conditions.

I walked aimlessly each night and day with no real direction and no sense of purpose.

My entire life is merely an insignificant piece of existence whose looming absence would offer no influence to the workings of the universe.

I merely continued to exist until the day comes when it'll be my turn to have my body laid to rest and my bones turned into dust.

That fateful day would come amidst the presence of another hapless rain.

One night, an unwavering pang of hunger struck me. I sat down on an empty bench placed right under a lamp-post.

I reached in within my plastic bag, knowing that I was reaching in for the last piece of bread I'd bought using the last of my money. But at that time, I didn't think much of it as I consumed the bread with so much gusto, consuming it at record time.

After that, I was still hungry.

Then I suddenly remembered that I still had a bottle of soda in the bag and it was half-full.

"Oooh, lucky," I thought as I excitedly unscrewed the bottle cap and hurriedly consumed the fizzy drink.

But as the liquid drained from the bottle, so did my feelings of euphoria. I slowly realized that it was my very last meal.

I looked around and noticed that the road and pavement I was on were devoid of any soul.

Across the street, there was a high-rise apartment building with all the lights turned on.

I could not see people anywhere, but the fact that all the lights were on gave me the sensible conclusion that everyone residing in it was happy and living well.

I was overwhelmed by feelings of sadness.

No, I didn't envy them. I know that every single person lives in the way that destiny has for them. But I couldn't quite gather from where those feelings of contempt were coming from.

Then the thoughts of that kidnapped girl entered my mind. I like to think that despite probably being forced to work as a prostitute, she was living a reasonably comfortable life.

It makes me smile to presume that she was taken under the wings of an old rich man and he was showering her with expensive gifts she would never be able to afford otherwise.

I guess it was appropriate to think of something pure and good as I begin to enter the final phase of my journey. But those are just my presumptions.

I've accepted that I would never get to find out what became of her. But if there is a speck of hope that the things I was imagining for her were a reality, then perhaps, my life isn't going to end on such a bad note.

I started to hear the faint sound of thunder from the distant heavens followed by the soft drizzle of rain slowly but deliberately touching my skin.

I reached into my garbage bag only to remember I'd also sold my worn-out umbrella. That's when I remembered that save for a rusty old knife; I have nothing left in it that holds any value.

The water from the rain and the coldness of the wind began seeping through my clothing. I remembered that man in the mountain again. I've finished off my version of his chocolate bar and found a comfortable place to succumb.

Like him, I was ready for the inevitable. But unlike him, no one would rescue me. And I would go ahead of him. A gleeful smile came across my face, knowing that I was not alone. I was experiencing the same death as those who braved the unforgiving mountains.

My eyes gave way as death started to cloak me under its loving embrace. My body started to stiffen from the cold then my mind wandered off for a bit.

"I'm glad I didn't have to use that dull, useless knife."

"That knife was supposed to be the replacement for the gun, wasn't it?"

"I did use it. I did. But not on me."

Sirens started blasting from a distance, followed by the panicked rush of vehicles. I opened my eyes enough to notice blood gushing from the plastic bag.

I peeked into the bag to inspect the lifeless head of a man sporting an ugly scar across his ugly face. Then I thought; that was it.

That feeling of content, calmness, and satisfaction towards the final moment in my life is the miracle that I was hoping for. And then…my body could no longer feel the cold. I could no longer feel anything.

"This is it," I thought.

That was the perfect way to go.

ABOUT THE AUTHOR

Frederick Trinidad

Frederick has been in the business of ghostwriting for a couple of years now. He wrote blogs for brands, web articles, social media posts, and scripts for different YouTube channels.

However, writing stories has been his passion since childhood and this anthology is his way of expanding his writing career and reaching a wide range of audiences. He discovered his love for horror storytelling during the peak of the pandemic when the world held its breath amidst a global state of uncertainty.

His innovative style of writing is designed to make readers experience his distinctive brand of horror and mystery for themselves.

Fred wrote a mystery/thriller novel that he works to see published by the first quarter of 2022. The short story contributions that he imparted in this anthology shall give you a peek at the horror that awaits you in that book and his literary works in the future.

To receive updates from his work, you can follow his personal Facebook account at:
https://www.facebook.com/frederick.trinidad.3

You can also reach him via email at: trinidadfred79@gmail.com

FOLLOW ME

By Chase Wilkinson

Party of the Century. That was what we called it. One for the ages.

None of us, not me, nor Sarah or Roger, had ever gotten that wasted before. Everywhere we looked, couples were making out, groups of seniors were playing beer pong and chugging some foul-smelling liquid that we'd never even seen before.

Some freshman had retreated to the backyard, sprawled over each other and comparing how queasy they felt. Empty wrappers, mixer bottles, and pizza crumbs covered the laminate flooring. We couldn't walk two feet without stepping in a puddle of wine or a pile of half-eaten Cheetos. It was disgusting, but we loved it.

It must have been past midnight; the roads were eerily quiet, dogs barked in the distance, but the loudest sound - by far - was the howl of the icy breeze that nipped at our ears and slashed our cheeks.

It was December.

Christmas time.

Neighbors welcomed the holiday season with poorly-built snowmen, cheap fairy lights, and shabby wreaths on their doors.

Wreaths represent eternal life in Christian culture. Sarah told me that. Our neighborhood was poorer than most; we celebrated as best we could, given the circumstances.

Roger was the poorest of us; he couldn't even afford a Christmas tree this year. His father is also an abusive, alcoholic scumbag that never worked a day in his miserable life - so there's that.

We happy few strolled gleefully through shin-high snow, giggling drunkenly to ourselves about whatever mischief we got up to at our freshman Christmas party.

In our defense, Christmas encourages underage drinking, so really, we're just victims of circumstance. Sarah, fair-haired and slender, held my hand as we walked. We had been dating for almost a year.

Roger, the singleton, never felt left out around us. He liked men. We've been best friends since childhood, so his sexuality wasn't a secret from me for very long. He trusted me. We all trusted each other.

Ahead, we reached our final destination as a threesome. This is the same spot where we always parted ways after school. Sarah and Roger lived on the east side of the estate, opposite me on the west side. Sarah gave me a farewell kiss, and Roger fist-bumped me.

"Be safe", Sarah said, and then we went our separate ways.

Perfect indentations of my feet marked my journey in soft patches of snow that crunched beneath my wellies. Somewhere, alley cats hissed and snarled as they fought over turf. Christmas decorations illuminated the pavement, guiding me home.

It may have been nearing one o'clock in the morning, but it had just occurred to me that the roads were almost too quiet. The entire west side was a ghost town, just like Silent Hill. Aside from Christmas lights, the streets were engulfed in darkness.

There were no streetlights on, nor any indoor lights. On a Saturday, this close to Christmas, you would think that at least a few houses on the block were celebrating until the early hours.

My footsteps quickened as a nauseating sense of foreboding and a surge of panic sobered me up from all the liquor.

Closer still, my front porch light was off. Whenever someone from our interconnecting neighborhoods - the west side and the east side - hosted a party, the parents of the attendees would leave their front porch lights on until their children got home safely.

Call it tradition, but our parents had always done it. My parent's light was off. Unless they had disowned me, that was unusual.

Suddenly, I'd become self-aware of my footsteps producing more sound than before. Their volume had doubled - double the impact and double the crunch. Not many safety videos actually told us what to do if we were being followed. My parents had sheltered me somewhat.

They had wrapped me in cotton wool for years, assuming that nothing bad could ever happen to me, so they never prepared me for such a scenario as this.

Running short on options, pure fear took over and my feet carried themselves faster, barely slower than a jog. Just get home.

Home is safe. No one can hurt you at home. Besides the heavier footsteps, seemingly doubled in loudness and intensity, the silence was broken by a blood-curdling scream.

It came from the east side, but it sounded close enough to have been right next to me. At this point, running was the only option. If

41

I'd reckoned, at the time, that the scream belonged to Sarah, I wouldn't have been so selfish.

Now, it didn't matter what other sounds were around. All I could hear was my own frantic breathing. I was asthmatic, so cardio was the last thing I should have been doing.

Reaching my doorstep, I fished for my keys in my coat pocket. Even with woolly gloves on, my fingers were trembling from the cold. It must have been minus degrees.

Finally, the keys granted me access and the door slammed behind me, putting a barrier between me and whoever - or whatever - had stalked me all the way home.

That night, my nightmares kept me wide awake. Like Nightmare on Elm Street, I thought that if I closed my eyes for even a split second, Freddy Krueger - or something worse - would come and get me. My parents slept through the commotion somehow.

The next morning, they made pancakes, but I wasn't hungry. My mother had quizzed me, but not about the fact that I was as white as a sheet, looking like I'd seen a ghost. Instead, she asked about Sarah and Roger and what shenanigans we had gotten up to at the party.

It felt like an interrogation, like I was the guilty suspect in a terrible crime. Dismissing myself from the table, I packed my things and set out for Roger's house.

Halfway there, my phone buzzed. It was our freshman group chat. Usually, I wouldn't entertain the jokes and chit-chat, but a news broadcast that was the local talk of the town.

Its headline read: *"Local girl found stabbed in mysterious circumstances."* Then, it hit me. Faster than I'd sprinted last night, I raced to Roger's house.

He confirmed my worst suspicions. Sarah was dead.

As far as the reason for her death, it was ruled as a suicide. There were no signs of physical assault or a struggle, but I knew better than that. Sarah was never unhappy, not so much so that she would take her own life. We were in love.

That day, Roger consoled me as I wept for Sarah's loss. He reassured me that there were "plenty of fish in the sea", but the only fish I wanted was dead.

When the dust had settled and my initial grief had passed enough for me to make intelligent conversation, I shared with Roger what I had experienced.

To my surprise, he told me that after walking Sarah to her house, he had continued on his own and the same thing had happened to him. He had an unsettling feeling that someone had followed him. His parent's porch light was off. We shared theories on what it could possibly be, but all sensible conclusions escaped us.

After bidding farewell to Roger, I set out, apprehensively, to return home and share the horrifying news with my parents. They were always behind with the times and hopeless with technology.

Halfway there, it was as if the previous night had repeated itself. Below zero temperatures froze my tears before they could even drop, but my sobs were silenced by that daunting sound of snow crunching behind me.

It had dawned on me that the stranger, whoever it was, must have tracked my movements and followed me - all day. The realization also struck me that this person was the same one that murdered Sarah, which made it increasingly likely that I was next.

All the sensible bones in my body suggested doing the same thing as before and outrunning the perpetrator, but that technique was predictable and it would only last so long.

Recalling what had happened to Sarah, it seemed necessary to confront whoever it was, but while that would be unexpected, it was also wildly idiotic. Still, never let it be said that I wasn't courageous.

Sarah would be proud. As the distance between me and my house lessened, the footsteps - the ones that doubled mine - grew louder than before. I felt a chilling breath on the back of my neck, even though I was speed-walking.

Making the worst decision, I stopped in my tracks. They stopped too. All was silent once more in our dull neighborhood. Come to think of it, I hadn't seen many people wandering about, even though it was Christmas Eve.

My phone buzzed. It was the freshman chat. An over-achieving nerd, Archie, had posted an updated image regarding Sarah's murder. She had taken a photograph just before her death, but the photograph baffled me - and all of us - because she had taken a picture of herself. She was holding the knife. That wasn't even possible.

Another icy breath chilled me to the bone. "Charlie", a menacing voice whispered, but I never turned.

My feet stayed firmly planted in a ditch of snow. How did they know my name? Worse yet, they sounded just like me.

My hands trembled. I opened my phone camera, pointing it back in the hopes of snapping an incriminating picture of this lowlife stalker. When the camera flashed, nothing appeared in the preview except more footsteps beside mine. They weren't my own. I was capable of making two steps at a time, but there were four tracks side-by-side.

"Charlie", the voice called, again. It was deeper, more demanding than before. All I could think about was how it sounded like me.

I should have run. I could have run, but I didn't. I stood there, like a lamb ready for slaughter. I thought of Sarah and how frightened she must have been. It broke my heart, but I was too scared to be upset.

My feet were glued to the spot. Without much else to keep me positive, I had accepted my fate. I had no weapon, I couldn't outrun them forever, so I turned.

If I was going to die, I wanted to know who my killer would be. When I turned, the shock of what I saw made my muscles spasm. My phone camera flashed, capturing the guilty party in a permanent image. It was me.

I was covered in blood, smiling sadistically from ear to ear. It was me, but it wasn't me. It was something evil. A burnt wreath was hanging around its neck - eternal life.

Before I could even register my own sickening reflection, a knife plunged through my stomach. It was cold, colder than the snowflakes that speckled my fringe, colder than the harshest winter.

That Christmas, I was fifteen. I had so much more life to live, but it was taken from me - by me.

ETHEL

By Chase Wilkinson

The countryside breathes in prospective tourists and exhales agronomists, permanently changed by the landscape design. In its midst, a frail sixty-something, skinny and disheveled, reclines by the crackling fireplace, holding an old black and white family portrait of herself, her ex-husband and their late daughter.

The face of the ex-husband is scribbled out with permanent ink. She trembles as the shattered glass frame is lifted toward the artificial light, glaring down at these forgotten few.

An age-old tale of an abusive husband and tragic miscarriage complete her harrowing backstory. She was young - twenty-three to be exact - and prosperous and in love.

Naivety does not escape the youths; she believed that she had found her Prince Charming. It all started several months after the engagement announcement. He was sweet at first; humble, loyal, romantic, but all of that changed when he began to grow restless.

He was older, thirty-five, and itching to leave the legacy of a family behind. He demanded a child, but while he wanted a daughter, Ethel, at foolish twenty-three, wanted a son. She could barely take care of herself, much less a child.

Not a day went by that he didn't beat her. She suffered horrendously by his hand. Meanwhile, pregnancy after pregnancy, she could only provide a son; for every gender reveal that determined a male, she would receive an assault and the demand of an abortion.

In the end, five children were conceived and all five were lost. Each one broke her heart and shattered her soul, but her husband-to-be saw only disappointment in every terminated child. After years of trying, at thirty-five years old, Ethel gave birth to a beautiful baby girl.

For months following her birth, the abuse stopped. They raised their child together, putting aside their petty differences, only for her to die prematurely at just five-years-old. Complications with her lung development had finally caught up to her, and soon enough, it killed her.

Ethel was inconsolable, but her husband was even more so. He would unleash his rage on her, and so the inhumane treatment continued.

Ten years passed. Ethel, now forty-five, outgrew her tolerance and gained some self-respect. She murdered the worthless low-life in cold blood following the final assault - the last time he would ever lay his hands on her.

Law enforcements ruled it as self-defense and that was all. Ethel became the notorious "husband killer" to the nosy neighbors that mysteriously stopped visiting her or delivered baked goods on ceramic plates. They were terrified of her; and rightly so. Ethel mourns her daughter endlessly; a mother's love is eternal.

Present day, Riley Thompson, nineteen, slim figure and carrying a hefty baby bump, strolls toward Ethel's quaint little cottage. In the front yard, a "for sale" sign sticks out from a neglected garden.

Christopher Morris, takes out one of his earphones. Chris is lean, athletic, pale faced and on the muscular side. They had discussed moving out together, starting a family, so before long, they were in search of their forever home.

"Your mom didn't seem happy with you movin' out", Chris remarks, "She practically kicked you out."

Riley sighs, forlorn, looking tired and worn out. Her complexion is pale and early wrinkles and grey hairs have aged her several years. Her curly hair is pinned up in a messy bun.

"She'll come around eventually," Riley counters, "I guess she wasn't ready for a grandson yet."

Riley is conventionally attractive, despite the flaws caused by morning sickness and sleepless nights. Chris nods knowingly and puffs on a cigarette.

"Uh-huh. She watched her little girl grow up. I know how it is." Chris has the characteristics - both physically and mentally - of a typical high school jock, which would make Riley his pretty, popular, self-centered valedictorian.

Inside the dilapidated cottage, the walls are moldy and rotted; the plastering has holes, the wallpaper has peeled and withered and the furniture is torn or dirty. Ethel, stirring a teacup, has a scar across her left eye spanning from her nose to her hairline.

Her face is blank. Surprisingly alert in her old age, she stares impatiently at a ticking clock on the mantelpiece.

An estate agent called that same morning, forewarning her of the guests that would be shortly arriving to examine her not-so-humble abode.

All is silent besides the crackle of flames, the crisp "chink" of metal hitting ceramic and the agonizing tick-tock of the old-timey clock.

Riley leers down at the rows of houses, then spots the isolated cottage at the far end. "This place is a little spooky," she says, no word of a lie.

"Don't you think? Mr. Parker from the housing agency wasn't kidding when he said that this neighborhood was "quiet and secluded"." Chris seems unfazed.

He has weathered far worse than a cranky old lady and a musty cottage. He acknowledges Riley and expresses his sympathetic affection by pulling her close as they walk side-by-side. Finally, they reach the end of the estate.

The house appears smaller from the outside. The garden is overgrown with pieces of broken gnomes scattered in the grass. A "FOR SALE" sign is embedded at an angle into the soft ground. The paint has been chipped away and cobwebs cover some of the letters. Chris crushes his cigarette bud under the heel of his boot.

"This must be the place, but you didn't put "haunted house" in the search bar by accident, right?" His poor attempt to lighten the mood is ill-fitting.

Riley, clearly disappointed by the layout of the house, half-smiles at such awful comedic timing. "Har-har. Very funny. This was the cheapest place on the market, it's not gonna be a cosy chalet."

Ethel cocks her head. Her hearing fails her in these golden years, but she can hear muffled voices coming from outside. From her seat, she can see through the gap in the drawn curtains.

Riley and Chris, living the fairytale romance that she could have only dreamed of, clear the cobblestone path to approach the front door. Riley's shirt is stretched out over her bulging stomach, indicating to Ethel that she is with child.

Given the sheer number of failed pregnancies and experience as a birth-giver herself, Ethel also knows that Riley is close to bursting. Any day now, that child will be born. Ethel stops stirring and squints through a gap in the half-open blinds.

Chris shoves his hands into the pockets of his leather jacket and hunches his shoulders, rightly commenting, "Jesus, it's cold out."

And it was. It was October. Halloween was but two weeks away, and even though it was still the cusp of winter, the temperature had plummeted. A mother and her toddler, roughly four-years-old, walk past the rickety building on their daily route.

The young boy reaches for a daffodil in Ethel's front garden. The mother looks cautiously at the house, then, feeling a sense of foreboding takes her son's hand and hastily quickens her pace.

Riley stares after them, confused and alarmed. When Chris speaks, it draws her out of her rampant thoughts. "Are we makin' a move or what?"

He can be so clueless - so oblivious - that it makes Riley wonder how they ever get along. Their personalities clash in every way.

"I'm starting to think there's a reason why this place had such a low price," Riley mentions, just as Chris observes the upside-down Christian cross above the doorway.

He knocks with a sturdy hand. When the decaying door creaks open, it sounds like a ghostly shriek - enough to chill Riley's bones for the second time that day.

The hallway is dark, and Ethel is almost invisible amidst its cloak of blackness. Chris can see some distinguishable features, captured in an unflattering light. Ethel is undoubtedly unpleasant to look at; she has wrinkles, scars and appears to be all skin and bone.

Chris spares a thought to wonder when the last time would be that she had eaten a nutritious meal. Overall, Ethel has an unwelcoming, hostile presence. A horrible smell wafts out from the eerie lair. It makes Riley cough violently.

All the while, Ethel's face remains deadpan. Emotionless. Chris blames it on dementia or some other degenerative disorder. Riley and Chris exchange looks, baffled by her lack of hospitality.

If she wanted to sell the property, which was unappealing to say the least, it would be expected that her demeanor would be less "living ghost" and more "friendly host", but it wasn't. They expected more of a welcome, or at least a reaction.

"Erm...hello. Did Mr. Parker tell you that we were coming? We came to look at the house," Chris begins, unsure of how else to engage Ethel without insulting the property or its owner.

Without proper warning, Ethel slams the door in their faces. Chris, reasonably shocked, splutters "What the fuck?" and persistently knocks again.

Considering the distance, he was unwilling to sacrifice the property after a three hour drive purely down to stubbornness.

When Ethel blatantly ignores the knock, he tries the doorbell. When Ethel is all but unresponsive, Chris calms his fruitless attempts at gaining her attention.

He says, "That was just rude. Are you sure we got the right place?" Riley chooses to ignore any further pursuit of the cottage and tugs at his sleeve as a wordless plea to leave.

"Forget it, Chris. I wanna go."

Chris complies reluctantly and they turn to leave. Clearly annoyed from discovering that Ethel is nothing but a time-waster, Chris kicks a shard of cracked terracotta clay with the rosy cheek of a garden gnome painted on it.

When they reach the gate, the door creaks open. Ethel is standing there, silently. Lifting his head, Chris shoots his mouth immediately.

"Hey, lady! Who do you think-" But it all happens quickly - too quickly.

In the blink of an eye, Ethel is sprinting at them, snarling like some rabid animal, knife in hand, with an impossible speed that a senior citizen could never possess. They turn to run, but she viciously stabs Chris' leg.

Riley shrieks and tries to clumsily catch him as he crumples. Ethel pries the "FOR SALE" sign from the dirt with unrealistic strength and swings blindly. Riley goes down hard and blacks out.

When she awakens, Riley's ears are ringing. She fades in and out of consciousness. Her stomach is throbbing. She groans, clutching the bump in agony.

Down there, in that basement, she is surrounded by corpses, relatively fresh. Some have cuts and bruises, others have large gashes. They are all women and all pregnant.

Riley recoils and hyperventilates from sheer terror. Tears fall, and she chokes on them. "Chris! *CHRIS!*"

"Oh my god, Chris, Chris!" Riley stares - wide eyed and fear-stricken - at the bounty of bodies.

From a dimly-lit corner, Ethel emerges from the darkness, a portrait of mania with her twisted features and soulless stare. Her eyes are black as night, veins bulging from her skinny, sun-spotted arms and creased temples. Old ladies are relatively sweet and pure, but not her.

Half an hour later, the front door opens. Ethel heaves as she drags out the "FOR SALE" sign and impales the ground with it.

She leaves it there, ready for the next takers.

ABOUT THE AUTHOR

Chase Wilkinson

 For over 7 years, Chase has been a noteworthy presence within creative media. As a self-proclaimed geek and driven by a passion for horror, comic books, video games, and modern cinema, she takes pride in providing only the best publications.

She likes to label herself as an innovative writer doing what she loves, especially when it concerns her favorite interests. Aside from personal written projects, she can be credited as an award-winning screenwriter, published poet, and accomplished academic writer.

They have taken the media industry by storm, producing short stories, screenplays, articles, features, and poetry that thoroughly engage, excite and thrill those fortunate enough to read them. They enjoy watching anime, horror movies, and animated shows; their life revolves around cinema, video games, and

Chase can be reached on: Instagram @chaseswilkinson.

Alternatively, they can be contacted via email: chasesidney32@gmail.com

CHECK OUT THESE TITLES

Creepy Nightmares

Scary Short Stories For Teens Book 1, 2 & 3

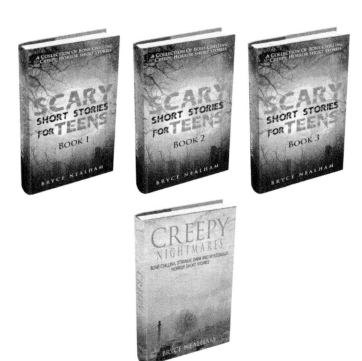

MORE CREEPY BOOKS
COMING SOON!

Printed in Great Britain
by Amazon

43802117R00036